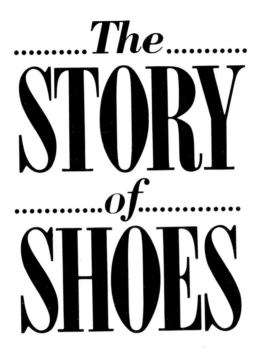

The STORY of SHOES

by Lucy Straus

illustrated by
Mas Miyamoto

STECK-VAUGHN
C O M P A N Y
A Subsidiary of National Education Corporation

Grass feels good on your feet. Sand feels good on your feet. It is nice to have no shoes on. But most of the time, you need shoes on your feet.

Today, you can get shoes when you need them. You can get all kinds of shoes. You can get them in shoe stores.

But long ago, there were no stores for shoes. Very long ago, there were no shoes at all!

We do not know just when the first shoes were made. But it was a long, long time ago.

Go back in time, way, way back. Your feet are cold. You need to warm them up. So you take a piece of animal hide. You put the hide on your feet.

Your feet are warm. But now you need to make the animal hide stay on your feet. So you use a vine to tie the hide on your feet.

That may be how some of the first shoes were made.

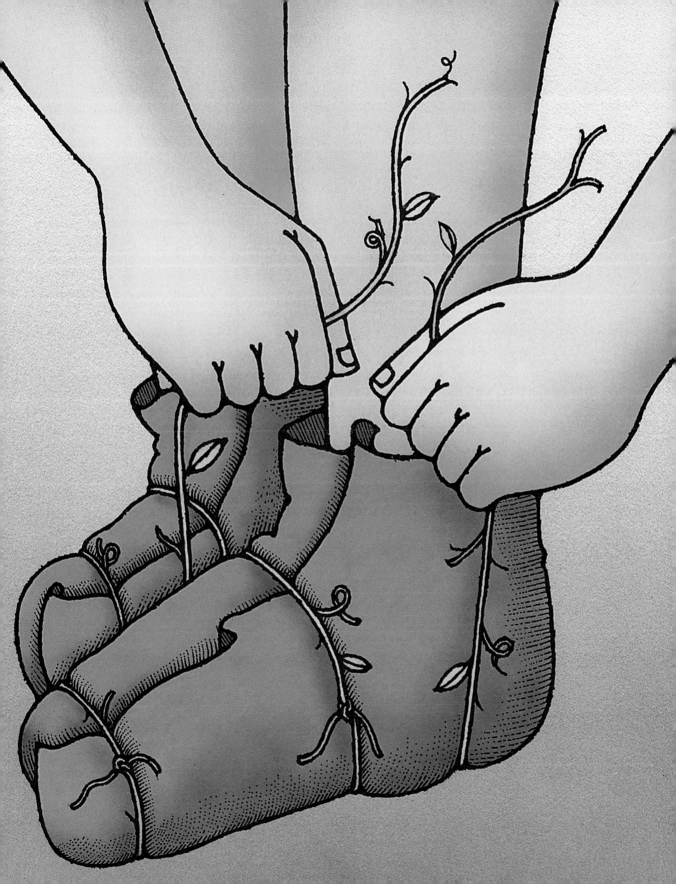

Long ago people in Egypt were wearing
sandals. Sandals are good for walking in hot
and sandy places.

Egypt is a very hot, sandy place. People in
Egypt were wearing sandals more than 4,000
years ago! Today, people in Egypt and other
warm places still wear sandals.

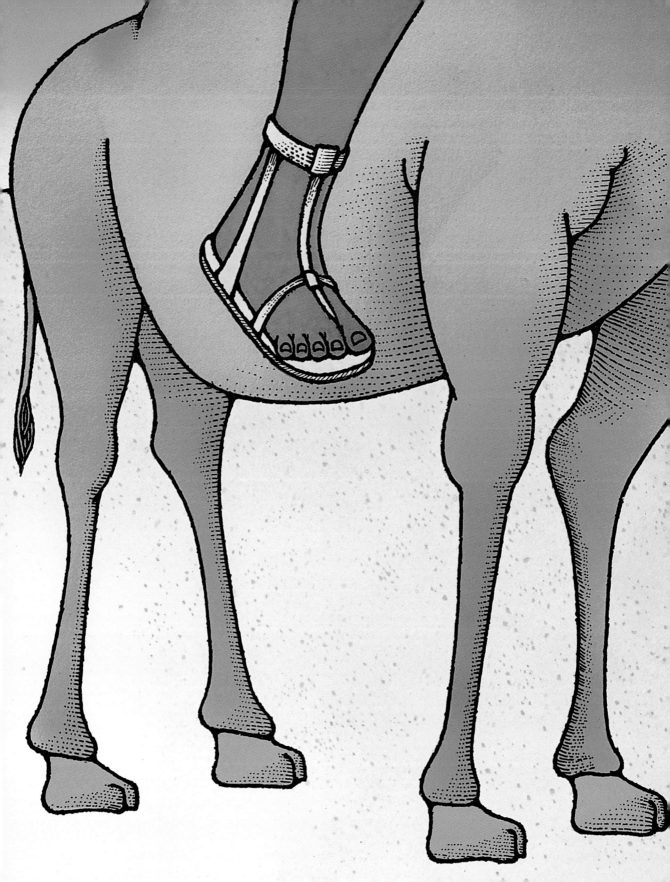

When it's cold, you need a closed shoe to keep your feet warm. Scotland is a place that sometimes is very wet and cold. About 3,000 years ago, people in Scotland were wearing boots. The people tied the boots to their feet. That way, the boots did not fall off.

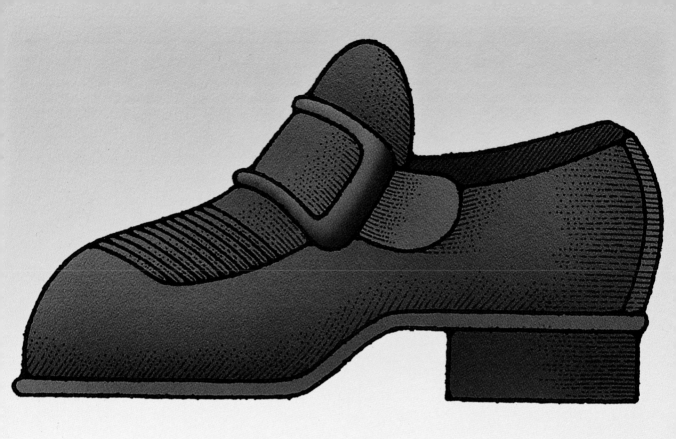

In time, there were many kinds of shoes.
Some shoes were made of wood. Some shoes
were very, very high and hard to walk on.

In the 1300s, the toes of shoes had very long
points. Sometimes people had to tie the ends
of the points to their legs so that they could
walk! In the 1500s, shoes had very wide
toes. These shoes look funny to us today.

14

Where did people get shoes long ago?

For a long time, most people would go to a shoemaker to get shoes. Shoemakers worked in little shops.

If you went into a shoemaker's shop, there might be some shoes there in the shop. But the shoes might not be the right size. You might need to have the shoemaker make shoes in the right size for you. That could take a long time. Back then, shoemakers had to make shoes one by one.

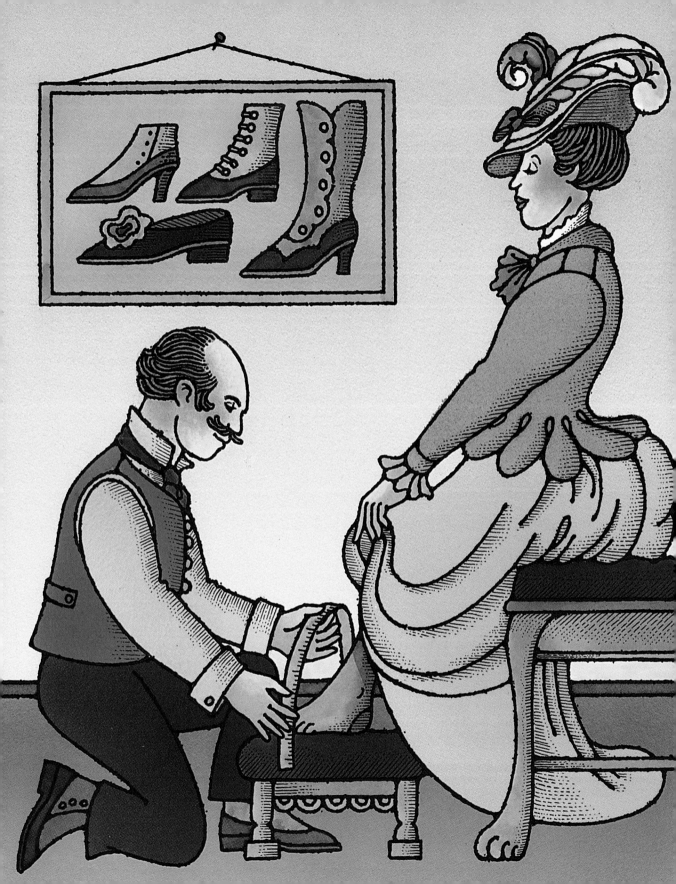

How did the shoemakers make the shoes?

The first thing a shoemaker needed to make shoes was a last. A last is a block of wood shaped something like a foot.

Lasts were made in different sizes for different feet. There were big lasts for big feet and little lasts for little feet. The shoemaker would start to make shoes by finding the right size last for the shoes.

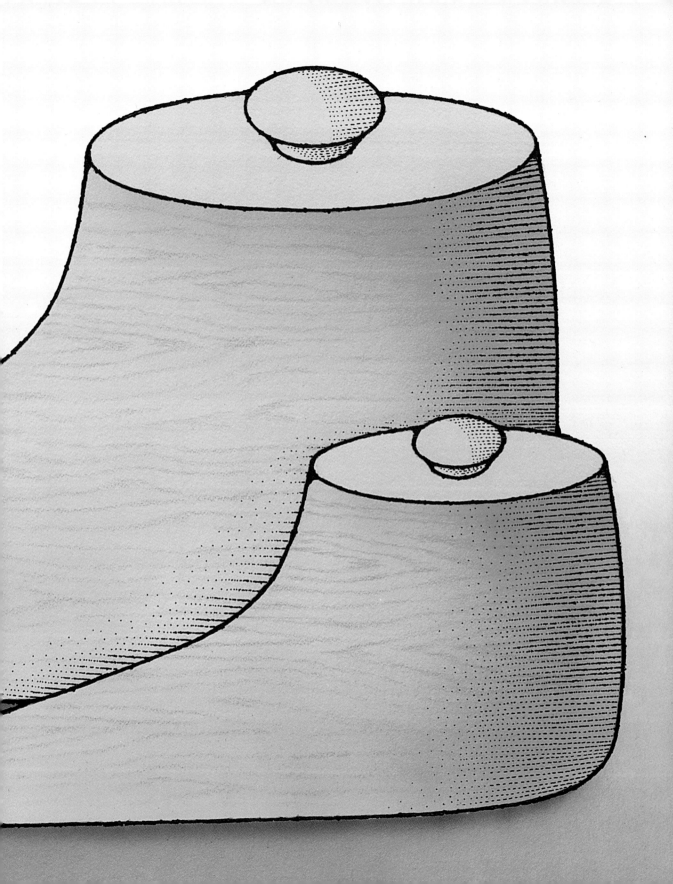

When shoemakers had the size last they needed, they would take leather and put it in water to make it soft. Then they would cut out some pieces of leather. One piece would be for the top of the shoe, and one would be for the bottom.

The shoemaker put the pieces of leather on a last to shape them into a shoe. Then the shoemaker would sew the pieces together. That is how shoemakers made shoes.

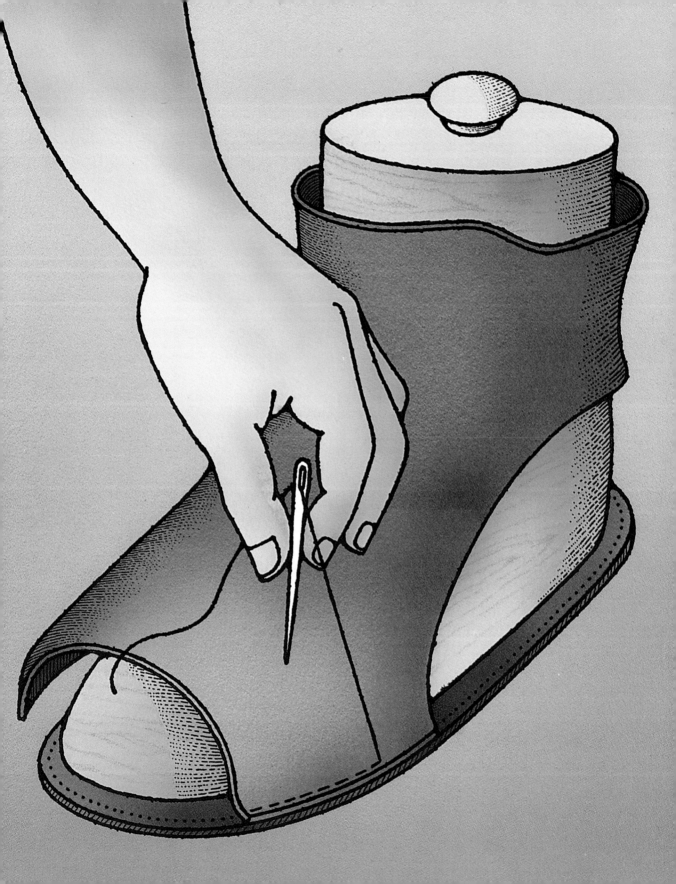

As time passed, shoemakers found ways to make shoes fit better.

Left feet and right feet look different. But before 1818, shoemakers used the same last to make shoes for left and right feet. That means that the shoe for the left foot was just the same as the shoe for the right foot. These shoes did not fit well!

Then in 1818, shoemakers started to use different lasts for left shoes and right shoes. People liked these new shoes. They fit so well!

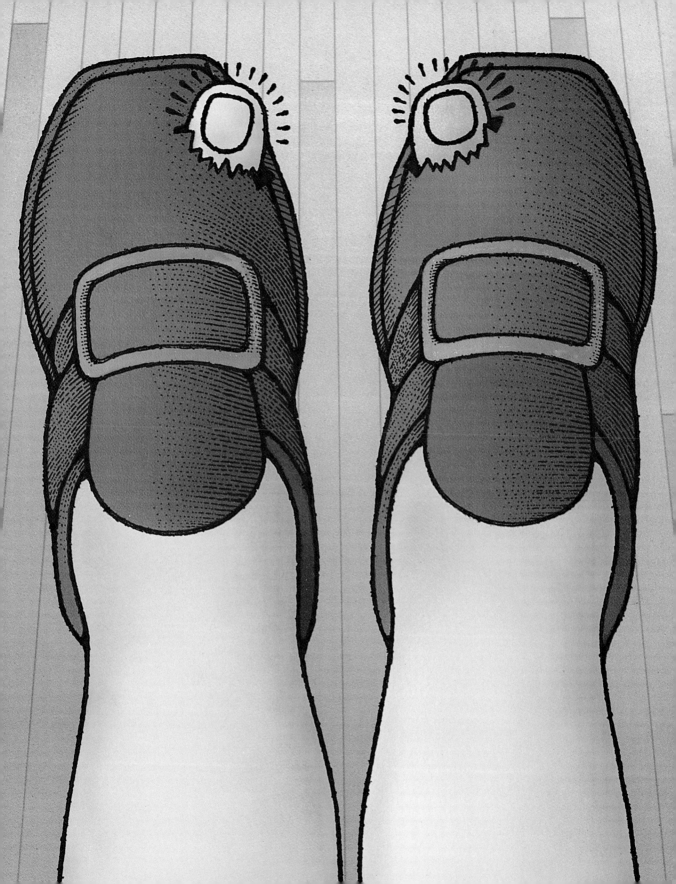

About the time that shoemakers started to make shoes fit better, they found new ways to make shoes, too.

Shoemakers found out that they did not have to make shoes one by one. Sometimes, shoemakers would work together.

One shoemaker would cut out the shapes. One shoemaker would shape them on the last, and one shoemaker would sew the leather together. That was how the first shoe factories began.

After the first sewing machine was made
in 1851, factories could make more shoes
than before. Sewing machines could sew
shoes fast.

Shoe stores got shoes from the factories. People
did not have to wait for a shoemaker to make
their shoes. They could go into a shoe
store and get shoes that were the right size.

Today, most shoes are made in big factories.
The people in the factories use many
different kinds of machines to make shoes.
There are machines to cut, machines to
shape, and machines to sew. Now people
can make lots of shoes at the same time.

Look down at all the feet when you walk.
Do you see boots? Do you see work shoes?
Do you see shoes with high heels? Do you
see sneakers?

Today, when you go into a store, you can
see many different kinds of shoes. You can
pick out the shoes that are just right for you!

Sharing the Joy of Reading

Beginning readers enjoy reading books on their own. Reading a book is a worthwhile activity in and of itself for a young reader. However, a child's reading can be even more rewarding if it is shared. This sharing can enhance your child's appreciation— both of the book and of his or her own abilities.

Now that your child has read **The Story of Shoes**, you can help extend your child's reading experience by encouraging him or her to:

• Retell the story or key concepts presented in this story in his or her own words. The retelling can be oral or written.

• Create a picture of a favorite character, event, or concept from this book.

• Express his or her own ideas and feelings about the subject of this book and other things he or she might want to know about this subject.

Here is a special activity that you and your child can do together to further extend the appreciation of this book: You and your child can design shoes for each other. Start by tracing the outline of one of your child's shoes (sideways) to get the shape of the shoe on $8\frac{1}{2}''$ x 11'' paper or brown-paper grocery bags. Have your child do the same with one of your shoes. Then use crayons or markers, fabric, glitter, glue, shoelaces, and string or other materials to create a pair of fantastic shoes for your child while your child creates shoes for you. You can cut out your finished designs and display them in your home.